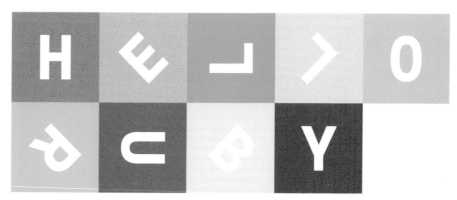

Adventures in Coding

Linda Liukas

Feiwel and Friends
New York

For Mom

This book wouldn't exist without the Kickstarter community
who helped me turn my dream into a reality.

A FEIWEL AND FRIENDS BOOK
An Imprint of Macmillan

Library of Congress Cataloging-in-Publication Data is available.
ISBN 978-1-250-06500-1 (hardcover) / ISBN 978-1-250-08088-2 (ebook)
Book design by Eileen Savage
Feiwel and Friends logo designed by Filomena Tuosto
First Edition—2015
The artwork was created in Photoshop using brushes developed by Kyle T. Webster.
The texture comes from a close-up photo of an old MacBook circuit board.
1 3 5 7 9 10 8 6 4 2
mackids.com

Introduction for the Parent

The idea for *Hello Ruby* was born in 2009, when I myself was learning to program. Whenever I ran into a problem, I would ask myself how a small, fierce girl would tackle it. But it took until the fall of 2013 for me to decide to be a children's book author. Since then, understanding technology through play, imagination, and creation has become my passion.

We all have stories that shape the way we see the world as adults. Like invisible friends, our childhood stories stay with us and influence our tastes for years to come. I think we need more of these voices and stories that are able to reveal the playful side of code.

Play is at the core of learning. Coding is like crayons or LEGO blocks—a way to express yourself. This book is not about "learning to code." It doesn't teach any specific programming languages, but introduces the fundamentals of computational thinking that every future kid coder will need.

Kids will learn how to break big problems into small problems, look for patterns, create step-by-step plans, and think outside the box. With activities included in every chapter, future kid coders will be thrilled to put their own imaginations to work.

Each chapter is a small story in Ruby's world, nine small lessons in computational thinking.

This book is designed to be worked on together with a parent. You can start by reading the entire story, or focus on one chapter at a time. Each chapter has a set of exercises that build on the concepts of play and creativity. Spend time playing and replaying the exercises. It's normal and okay to make mistakes and to look at the same problem in different ways. That's all part of computational thinking.

Toolboxes give additional information for parents and list concepts that are linked to the topic discussed. All concepts can be found in the glossary. You can also find suggested answers in the answer key at helloruby.com. There, you'll also find more play activities and fun things to do, and you can see what other kids have created all around the world!

Ruby and Her Friends

Ruby

About me: I like learning new things and I hate giving up. I love to share my opinions. Want to hear a few? My dad is the best. I tell great jokes. I'm a mischief-maker and prefer my cupcakes without strawberries, please.

Birthday: February 24

Interests: Maps, secret codes, and small talk

Pet Peeves: I hate confusion.

Favorite Expression: Why?

Secret Superpower: I can imagine impossible things.

Penguins

About us: We're very smart. But occasionally others think we're eccentric. We communicate with very short (and often rude) sentences. We love problems—especially breaking them into smaller pieces.

Birthday: August 25

Interests: Patterned knits, riddles, and abbreviations

Pet Peeves: We hate being told what to do. And spaghetti.

Favorite Expression: Have choices.

Secret Superpower: We're older than the others.

Django

About me: I have a pet snake called Python. I'm very organized, persistent, and somewhat rigid. I like things that can be counted: odd, even, prime, cubed, rooted, backward, and forward. But I don't take myself too seriously.

Birthday: February 20

Interests: The circus, philosophy, and pythonic things

Pet Peeves: People crowding around me when I stand in line

Favorite Expression: Simple is better than complex.

Secret Superpower: I always have a solution.

Snow Leopard

About me: I'm the most beautiful, polite, and well-mannered Snow Leopard I know. I often have fights with the Robots. (Which is kind of pointless, since we are similar in the end.)

Birthday:	June 8
Interests:	Solitude, Zen, and Pilates
Pet Peeves:	People think I'm tough, but I'm really cuddly.
Favorite Expression:	Think different.
Secret Superpower:	Boundless beauty

Robots

About us: We are playful and flexible and fast. We have hundreds of Robot siblings. We're never happier than when we're all building something together.

Birthday:	September 23
Interests:	Cooking shows, the Penguins, and making more friends
Pet Peeves:	We don't get all the fuss about being clean and consistent. Who cares?
Favorite Expression:	Be together.
Secret Superpower:	We might look small, but we grow up really fast.

Foxes

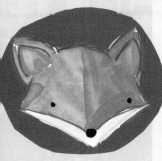

About us: We get really excited about new things. We love gardening and grow many kinds of plants and species (and sometimes bugs). We like being enthusiastic, friendly, and cheerful. But don't try to limit our freedom! (That's when we get really angry.)

Birthday:	November 7
Interests:	Gardening, geckos, and nighttime
Pet Peeves:	Always being safe!
Favorite Expression:	Let's do it!
Secret Superpower:	We can spin and somersault like no one else.

Ada &
Grace &
Frances.

Chapter 1: Meet Ruby

RUBY is a small girl with a huge imagination.

She loves to crawl under her bed and imagine all the bugs that might live there. She's always coming up with new dance moves, and her favorite word is "why."

In Ruby's world, she's the chief creator and architect. One day, she's a doctor, the next, a bug hunter. Her superpower? Ruby can build things with her imagination. Anything is possible if Ruby puts her mind to it.

One thing Ruby doesn't like is to be told what to do. Sometimes this means trouble—especially if the instructions are unclear.

When Ruby's dad asks her to get dressed for school, she puts on her dress and shoes, but keeps her polka-dot pajamas on. After all, Dad didn't tell her to first change out of her pajamas.

When it's time to clean up her toys, Ruby puts her stuffed animals, building blocks, and toy house away, but leaves her drawing pencils on the floor.

"Pencils aren't really toys," she says cheekily.

Chapter 2: The Clues

RUBY stomps and stumbles around her world while her dad is away working and traveling. Oh, how Ruby wishes she could go with him on his adventures. Working must be the best.

But just when Ruby really starts missing her dad, she finds something unexpected: a postcard. Ruby's dad is always full of great surprises!

POST CARD

Dear Ruby,

Today you're off on a grand adventure. I've hidden five gems for you to find. Keep going until you find them all. If you have more than one idea, follow the best one. And if you need help, remember that friends can often be found in unexpected places. I can't wait to hear how you found all the gems.

Kisses,
Dad

Little Miss Ruby

by the windowsill

Ruby is excited. She wants to start her adventure and find the gems, but Dad hasn't left any instructions. How absentminded of him! *Where should I begin? How do I find the clues?* she ponders.

Ruby feels like she could lie down and cry. But Ruby is a very practical girl, and she knows that often, big problems are just lots of little problems stuck together.

And with those thoughts in mind, she knows
what her first step should be. "I'll make a plan!"

Having a plan makes Ruby feel stronger. First, she slides under the desk to look for hints and finds four crumpled pieces of paper.

For someone else, these papers might look like trash—random numbers, words, and statements— but for Ruby they are clues. Like a secret code.

Snow Leopard lives
on a mountain = true.

Penguins live in a
house = false.

Steps south to Foxes
from Snow Leopard:
100 × 4

Address.
Robots = "1600
Amphitheatre
Parkway"

Greetings from
the river!

Chapter 3: Ruby's Plan

THE next thing Ruby needs is a map! Carefully, she marks a spot for the Penguins next to the riverbank, then she finds the address of the Robots and draws their tiny house. On the mountain, Ruby carefully writes "Snow Leopard," and then figures out where the Foxes live—in the little garden below the Snow Leopard.

3 FOXeS

4 RoBotS

5 Ruby's world

But the map is far from complete. Ruby doesn't have any idea where the fifth gem might be. And she has so many questions.

How do I find all five gems?

What happens if I get lost in the forest?

How do I know what to bring with me?

Ruby thinks long and hard. She decides that she'll just follow the shortest route from one place to another and marks the order of her visits. And she'll take a roll of rope with her. Rope always seems like a good idea. Maybe Dad left her help after all.

Ruby rolls the map into a tight little bundle and sets out into the unknown.

Chapter 4: The Penguins

THE first stop on the map is the home of the Penguins. Now, there's one thing Ruby knows about Penguins: They are very smart, but sometimes hard to understand.

Ruby approaches the Penguins and politely asks, "Have you seen a gem my dad could have hidden here?"

"Gem: a valuable stone that is cut and polished," the Penguin named Tux says solemnly.

"Bang splat tick tick hash," the Penguin with the scarf chimes in.

"False! My dad lives in the North Pole," concludes the chubbiest Penguin.

Ruby thinks about each of the answers—they almost sound like another language. She realizes she needs to be more specific when asking the Penguins her question. She tries again.

"Is there something smaller than my fist, cut of rock or mineral, of any color, and which is rarely seen here?"

"True!" yells the chubbiest Penguin as he merrily points toward the river.

"Oh, so the gem is in the river! Why don't we build a raft to try to get the gem out of the water?" Ruby suggests.

The Penguins agree and quickly organize themselves into a complex mission. They gather some sticks and Ruby lends her rope. Each little Penguin and Ruby does only one small task, but together they are powerful. In no time, the raft is ready, and together they push it out into the water to find the sparkling gem.

Chapter 5: Snow Leopard

WAVING good-bye to the Penguins, Ruby climbs to the next stop on her map: the top of the mountain. And who does she run into but the elegant Snow Leopard. Snow Leopard will surely be able to help her, but something is wrong.

"Why are you so upset?" Ruby asks.

"I live up here because I love things that are simple and tidy. And now there's disorder," scoffs Snow Leopard. "Look! It blinks! It's colorful and it hurts my eyes!"

Ruby glances in the direction Snow Leopard is pointing and sees a faint glimmer on the roof of Snow Leopard's home. "It's a gem!" Ruby cries out in delight. But Ruby is too small and the gem is too high up for her to reach.

"Focus on the pure things," Snow Leopard stoically advises. "Ignore the details that make things different. This will help you come up with a solution."

Ruby takes a moment to clear her mind. She spots a bunch of sticks on the ground. Last time, she made a raft with the Penguins to get to the river. Maybe she can use sticks and rope to make other things.

She builds a simple
structure of rope and sticks,

×5

repeats it five times,

and soon has a ladder.

Snow Leopard smiles (in that special way only Snow Leopards know how to). With the second glittering gem stowed away, Ruby thanks Snow Leopard and asks, "What is the best way to get to the garden?"

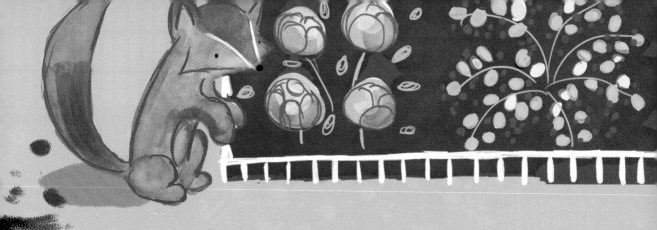

Chapter 6: The Garden

WHEN Ruby arrives, the whole garden is in chaos! Everything is out of order with dirt, vegetables, and Foxes flying every which way. It's hard to focus on anything. The Foxes are confused about what to do. They keep repeating tasks that are already done, and missing other jobs that need to be completed.

"New rule! New rule!" the boss Fox yells. "Everyone grab a seed to plant and at the same time weed the garden."

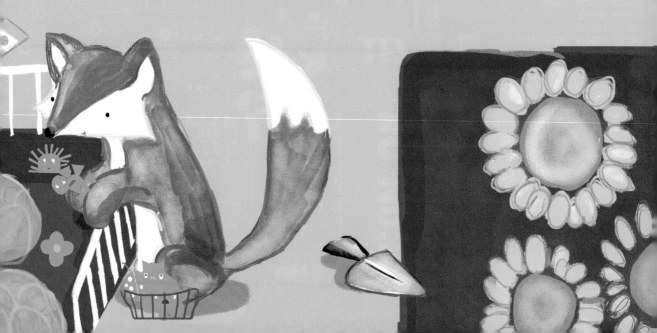

Ruby observes all the craziness and comes up with an idea. She raises her voice and gets everyone's attention. "You, you, and you—you're the planters. You need a bag of seeds. If the hole is empty, drop in one carrot seed. If there's already a seed, move on. Keep going until you hit the end of the row, then move to the next row. Repeat the whole thing five times."

Ruby is pleased with herself. Now, onto the others.

"The rest of you—you're the weeders. Your role is to remove everything green and living, unless it's a carrot seedling. Check each row. Stop when you've reached the end of the fifth row."

"Oh, that helps," says the boss Fox a little sheepishly.

Everyone gets to work. And just when it's
time to plant the last carrot seed, Ruby spots
something half-buried in the mud—it's a sparkling
pink gem! With three gems in her pocket, Ruby
lets out an exhausted but happy sigh. And that's
when she smells something sweet drifting through
the air. Her stomach starts to growl.

Chapter 7: The Robots

NOT too far away, in a very busy house with a very busy kitchen, the happy Robots are baking. It smells like candy canes, cinnamon, cookies, milk, and jelly beans. *A gem could easily be hidden in the messy kitchen*, Ruby thinks.

   The Robots love sharing everything, and they quickly invite Ruby in and teach her how to make cupcakes.

"Writing a recipe allows you to make many cupcakes. Once you've found a good recipe, you can make hundreds of cupcakes or you can swap ingredients and make many different kinds of cupcakes," explains one of the Robots.

"And recipes get better when you share them. You make friends when you share," continues the Robot with the chef's hat.

So Ruby makes cupcakes. Lots of cupcakes. When she's done, she picks one to take with her. "I'll take the cupcake that has red sprinkles, yellow frosting, and no strawberries," Ruby decides.

Ruby takes a final peek under the shelf and into the oven but is disappointed that she can't find the gem. With a cupcake in her hand, Ruby thanks the Robots and is on her way. When she takes a bite, she sees something inside the cupcake glimmer!

Chapter 8: Django

RUBY walks into the forest with the four gems in her backpack. Before she can get very far, a boy with a huge snake wrapped around his shoulders jumps out in front of her. Ruby spies the final gem in a chain around the boy's neck.

"Where did you get that gem? And what is that creature?" Ruby asks.

"My name is Django and this is my pet, Python. Who are you? What are you doing in my forest?"

"I am Ruby. This is not your forest. It belongs to everyone," Ruby says fiercely.

Ruby storms off without the gem, determined to get home and away from this boy, but when she reaches the riverbank, it is too wide for her to cross. Ruby stops to think. Surely she can figure this out.

"You're doing it wrong," says Django, sneaking up behind her. "Let me show you how."

"I know how to solve this myself," Ruby replies.

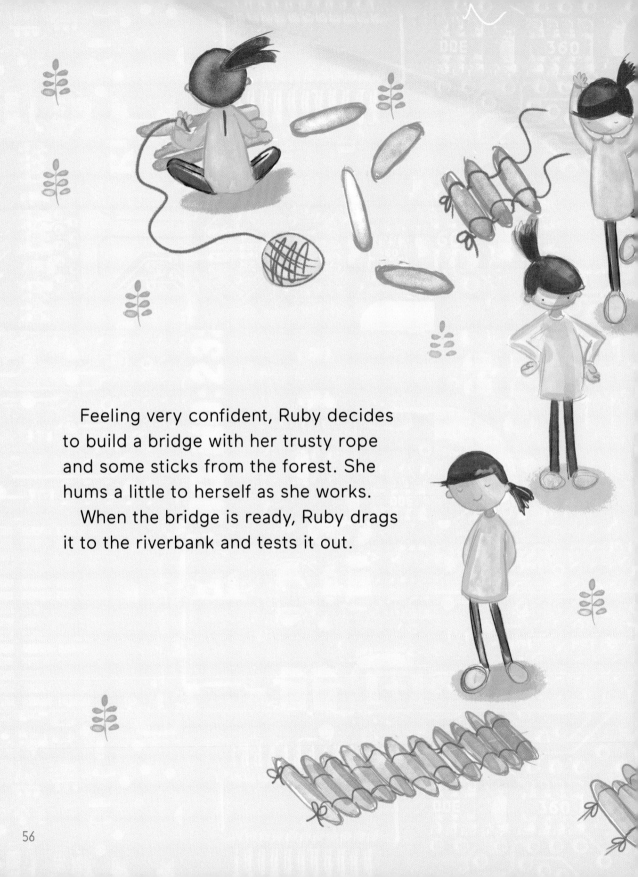

Feeling very confident, Ruby decides to build a bridge with her trusty rope and some sticks from the forest. She hums a little to herself as she works.

When the bridge is ready, Ruby drags it to the riverbank and tests it out.

But it doesn't work!

Chapter 9: The Problem

RUBY is embarrassed. In her rush to build the bridge, she had forgotten to think about how to fasten it to the other side of the river.

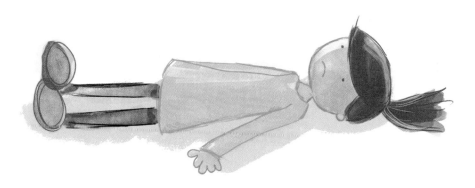

"It's okay, Ruby. That was a great first try,"
Django assures her. "We can figure this out
together. Do you still have rope left?"

"What if we use my rope to tie the bridge to
Python and he can swim it to the other side?"
Ruby suggests after thinking a while.

Their plan works!

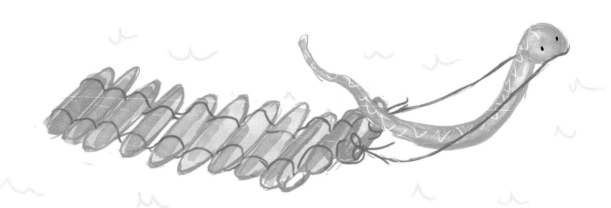

Chapter 10: Home

BACK in her own bed, Ruby thinks about the long day. She is almost asleep when dad walks in. "Dad, I found all the gems! I made a plan," Ruby starts sleepily.

"It wasn't perfect, but that's okay, because I got help from the curious Penguins and we built a raft together. Then, I met the lonely Snow Leopard, who taught me to focus and make a ladder. And I helped the gardening Foxes work better together and learned to bake the most delicious cupcakes with the Robots. Even bossy Django helped me."

"They're all so very, very different, but they all helped me on my adventure in some way, and they're all . . . friends."

Activity Book

There's one friend of Ruby's you haven't yet met. Say hello to the computer! The secret to know about computers is that they are really good—and fast!—at following instructions, but they can't really think for themselves.

You, on the other hand, have your own imagination and skills, so you'll have fun solving these activities. Let's go!

1
MEET RUBY

You just met Ruby. She's quite the girl, isn't she? The reason she isn't afraid to try new things is because she knows a secret: All big problems are just tiny problems stuck together. Sometimes the only way to learn something new is to make a lot of mistakes first.

Toolbox:

These exercises call out ways we can give exact instructions in our daily lives and help understand the importance of giving commands in the right order, recognize patterns, and know how to break things down. This information is important when talking to a computer.

Programming or coding is giving step-by-step instructions to a computer on what to do and in which order. Instructions need to be small enough for the computer to be able to understand them. They need to be clear and detailed. If not, the computer will make mistakes. Soon you'll learn to think about problems just like a computer would. That's called computational thinking!

| »Sequence | »Decomposition | »Pattern Recognition |

Bossy Little Ruby

Did you notice Ruby being a little cheeky while cleaning her room? She learned it from her computer. How would you instruct Ruby in the following situations? Take a piece of paper and write down the instructions for:

- Eating breakfast
- Making the bed
- Taking a nap
- Setting the table

Example: Ruby's instructions for brushing teeth

1. Walk to the bathroom.
2. Pick up your toothbrush and add one dollop of toothpaste.
3. Open your mouth and start brushing your teeth. Repeat until you have brushed all your teeth.
4. If you still have toothpaste in your teeth, take a sip of water. Else, leave the bathroom.

> Make sure you give instructions to me in the right order! I'm really quick and accurate when following instructions. When you write these step-by-step instructions, it's called coding!

 **Do it Yourself**

Find a friend—one person can act as Ruby, and the other person's task is to explain how to do the above things.

Start with eating breakfast. Break down the tasks into tiny, exact commands. The other person gets to be Ruby and try to misunderstand the commands. Then swap roles!

Builder

Ruby is really good at imagining and building stuff. It's easy, once you realize that all things are built out of smaller things.

Ruby builds . . .

. . . a bird. One piece is missing. Can you tell which one?

. . . a bug. Ruby can make this bug out of these pieces! But which piece won't she use?

. . . a processor. Which three pieces did she not use?

 Do it Yourself

Can you break down one of your own drawings? What are the different parts it's made of?

Ruby's Outfit Rules

Look at the clothes in Ruby's closet. Ruby is very particular about what she wants to wear. Point at the right outfits that match her rule:

- On Mondays I wear clothes with polka dots.
- On Tuesdays I wear blue or yellow clothes.
- On Wednesdays I choose only clothes that begin with the letter D.
- On Thursdays I wear hats.
- On Fridays I wear white and pink clothes.
- On weekends . . . Now it's your turn to decide Ruby's dress-up rule!

 You can print out Ruby paper dolls at helloruby.com.

2

THE CLUES

The world is full of all sorts of interesting things! Ruby found bits and pieces of data under her dad's desk, like an address for the Robots, the number of steps to get to Snow Leopard, and finally a sentence Ruby knew right away was not true. Let's take a look at some other interesting numbers and words.

Toolbox:

These exercises help in understanding the different types of data a computer uses to make and store things. In programming, this data is stored in a variable. Lots of things can be stored as variables:

- Strings, which include letters, numbers, spaces, and other characters on the computer keyboard wrapped in quotes. Like this: "Ruby"
- Numbers, such as 1, 2, 3, or 4.12.
- Booleans, which are expressions that are either "true" or "false"

» Strings   » Numbers   » Booleans

In a computer game, you could store data like your player name (string), how many points you've collected (number), and whether you've already completed the game (boolean).

Dad's keyboard

Ruby thinks Dad's keyboard is magical. But there's a secret to this keyboard:
The names of Ruby and five of her friends are hidden in it. Follow each color
to find the name of each friend. Once you've found a name, write it down on
a piece of paper.

 Do it Yourself

Some of the buttons are empty. Can you
design your own buttons? What would
they do? Can you write your own name?

You can print and design your
own keyboard at helloruby.com.

Ruby's Tea Party

Ruby loves organizing tea parties. But she needs your help! Can you help Ruby check that everything is in order for the party?

- Will everyone invited have a place to sit? Help Ruby count the guests.
- How many of Ruby's teacups are pink? How many are yellow?
- Which cake has more pieces, the orange cake or the green cake? Which has fewer? Count their sections to find out.
- Each friend wants to have two pieces of the orange cake. Is there enough of it?
- Which plate has the most things on it? Which has the fewest?

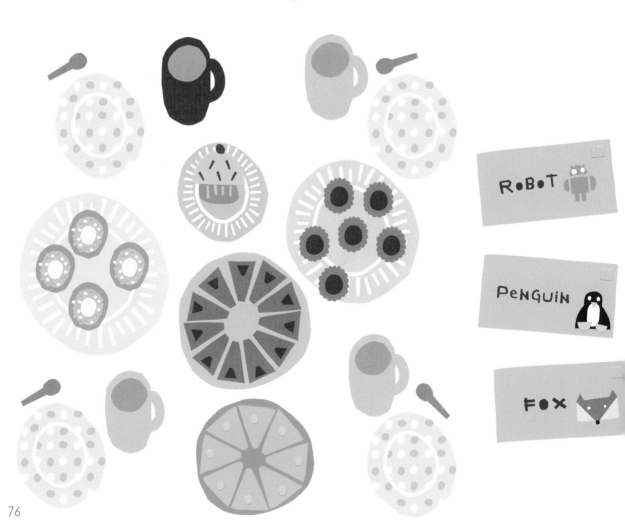

Truthsayer

Ruby likes to get to the bottom of things. Knowing what's true and what's false is another type of information. Can you help Ruby solve these puzzles? Which of them are true and which of them are false?

I'm red and yellow.   True/False
I'm pink and green.   True/False
I'm happy.   True/False

My eyes are green.   True/False
I have six points.   True/False
I am not yellow.   True/False

I have legs.   True/False
I have arms and legs.   True/False
I have arms or legs.   True/False

My secret trick? To know if something is true or false, pay close attention to the words *and*, *or*, and *not*.

BriLLiAnt

You can play this game with any of your toys. Come up with three things that are either true or false. Make them tricky! Ask a friend to guess which one is true.

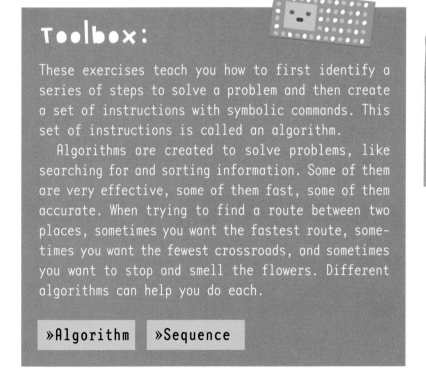

3

RUBY'S PLAN

Making a plan is fun! Even though Ruby doesn't know exactly what will happen, she has a step-by-step plan to solve the problem. Plans don't always work, though, and sometimes you need to think of a new plan. But it's still better to have a plan than to wander aimlessly around.

Toolbox:

These exercises teach you how to first identify a series of steps to solve a problem and then create a set of instructions with symbolic commands. This set of instructions is called an algorithm.

Algorithms are created to solve problems, like searching for and sorting information. Some of them are very effective, some of them fast, some of them accurate. When trying to find a route between two places, sometimes you want the fastest route, sometimes you want the fewest crossroads, and sometimes you want to stop and smell the flowers. Different algorithms can help you do each.

»Algorithm   »Sequence

Algorithm—wow, that's a big word—but all it really means is a step-by-step plan for getting something done. Computers like these steps to be written in symbolic commands—it's easier for us to understand.

Fabric Pattern

See if you can match the rule to Ruby's fabric patterns above. Now, find a piece of paper and see if you can follow the rules to make a different pattern for each algorithm.

Draw lines   Straight   Overlapping   Use three colors

Draw lines   Not straight   Not touching   Use four colors

Draw dots   Two different sizes   Use five colors

Draw lines   Zigzagged   Use two colors

Easy – peasy

Make a Map

Now it's your turn to help Ruby get to her friends. You can move Ruby with arrows up, down, right, or left. Take as many steps as you need. Once you've reached the block the friend is in, stop and say hello. Look out for the blue water (and use the brown bridge)!

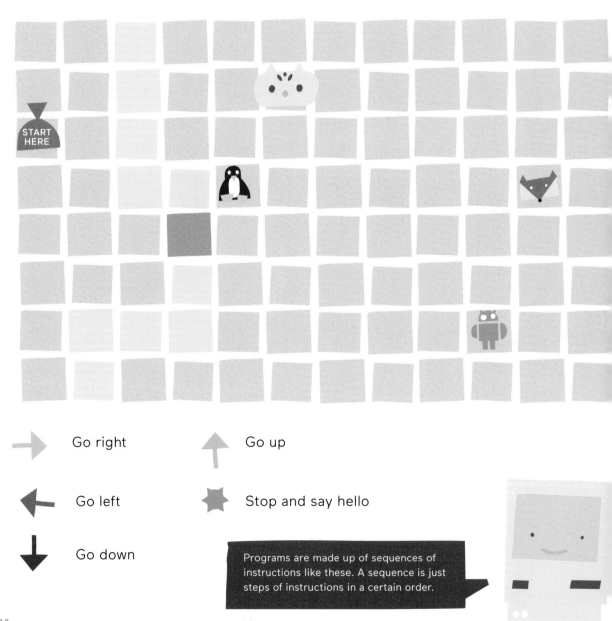

→ Go right

↑ Go up

← Go left

⭐ Stop and say hello

↓ Go down

Programs are made up of sequences of instructions like these. A sequence is just steps of instructions in a certain order.

- Write each step down with an arrow pointing to the right direction. Here is an example for how to get to the Penguins:

- Sometimes you need to draw a lot of arrows to get to a friend. Guess what? There's a shortcut! Instead of writing this:

- You can write this:

- They both mean three steps to the right. Now, the road to the Penguins looks like this:

Now, write down the instructions to get to Snow Leopard, the Foxes, and the Robots in the same way. Try writing the long version first, then figure out the shortcut.

Do it Yourself

Take a piece of paper and draw a map of the route from your home to school. Can you write the instructions to get there?

4
THE PENGUINS

When Ruby meets the Penguins, she learns that speaking the same language as them is the best way to give clear instructions. Now that Ruby is collecting more information, she needs to think of ways to keep everything in place. Ruby knows keeping things nice and tidy can sometimes be difficult!

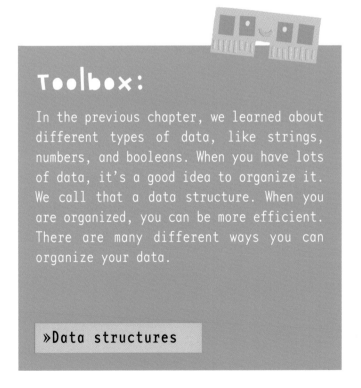

Toolbox:

In the previous chapter, we learned about different types of data, like strings, numbers, and booleans. When you have lots of data, it's a good idea to organize it. We call that a data structure. When you are organized, you can be more efficient. There are many different ways you can organize your data.

»Data structures

The Penguins have a secret language of their own. But I can understand it when I have a key like the one you see on the next page.

Secret Language

Can you read the Penguins' code? Use the chart below to decode their messages. Come up with a new message for the third Penguin!

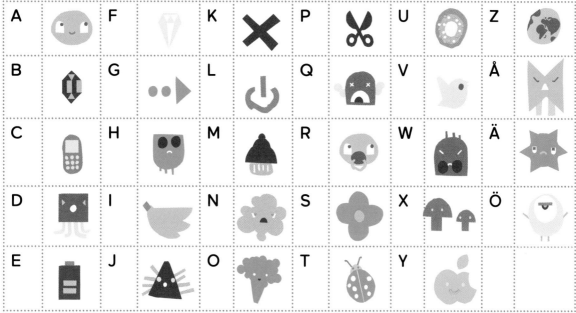

💡Do it Yourself

Can you write your name in the Penguin language? Or try writing a secret language of your own.

Lunchtime

Ruby needs to organize the lunchboxes for the Penguins. The Penguins are very particular about their food. Can you help her put the food below in the right compartments?

Each lunchbox is separated into four areas. Foods with things in common share the same section.

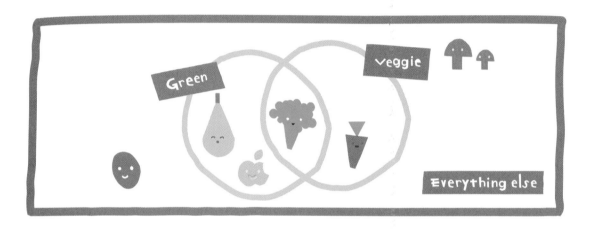

 Hint!

Food in the middle has things in common with food in both right and left lunchbox compartments.

Can you help Ruby sort Zip's, Seq's, and Popd's lunchboxes?

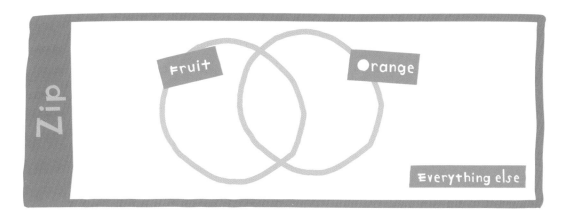

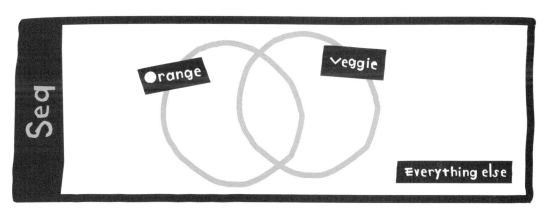

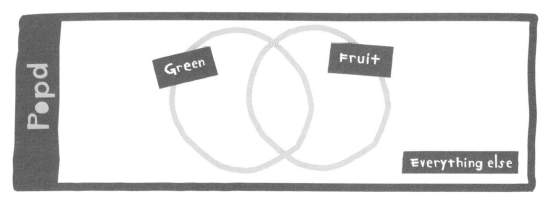

5
SNOW LEOPARD

Ruby has never met a cat quite as particular as Snow Leopard—she's very refined and doesn't like extra hassle. With the help of Snow Leopard, Ruby builds a ladder. Actually, she builds one step of the ladder and repeats it five times. That's called a loop.

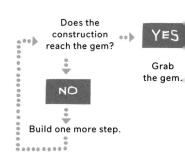

Does the construction reach the gem? → YES

Grab the gem.

NO

Build one more step.

Toolbox:

This chapter introduces the concept of a loop. Looping means repeating the same thing or set of things over and over again.

The simplest loops are ones that repeat a fixed number of times. Often, you'll need a loop to keep repeating until something changes: The thermostat will be off until the weather gets cold, or in a game, points are collected until the time is up. Sometimes loops run forever.

»Pattern recognition »Loops

I'm very good at repeating the same task over and over again without getting bored. I don't even need a lunch break! All I need to know is when to start, what to do, and when to stop.

Wallpaper

Snow Leopard is decorating her house with stylish wallpapers. Can you help her complete the pattern?

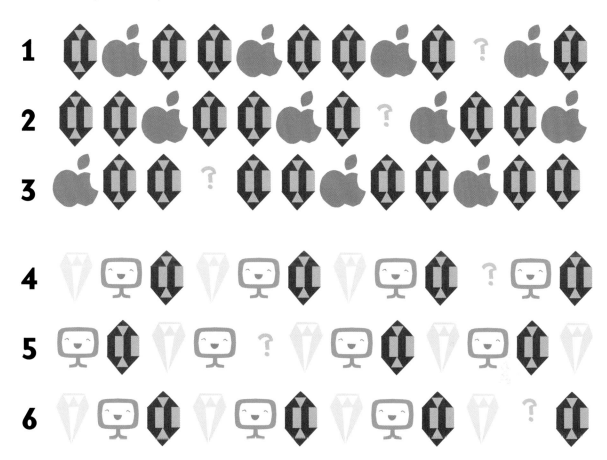

Do it Yourself

To make a loop, you need to first be good at spotting patterns. There's a loop in each row of Snow Leopard's wallpapers! Can you use your finger to trace a circle around the structure that repeats in the pattern? How many times does the loop happen?

Dance, Dance, Dance!

Put your dancing shoes on—let's have a party! Ruby and her friends like to dance. They all have their signature moves. Repeat after them! How many times can you do the dance routine? (Snow Leopard would call this a loop.)

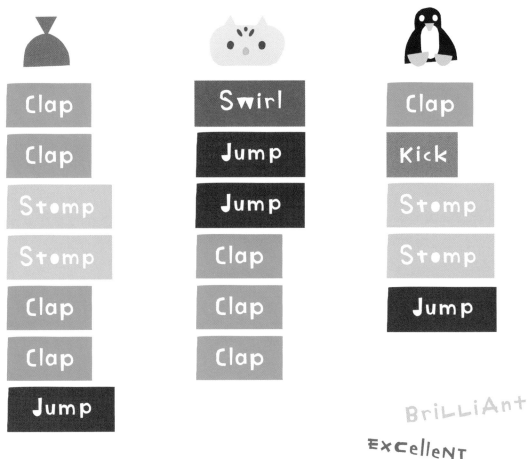

BriLLiAnt

EXCelleNT

Now it's your turn!

- **First round:** Repeat one dance routine three times.
- **Second round:** Choose one dance routine and repeat until your partner claps his or her hands together.
- **Third round:** Repeat Ruby's dance moves while your partner is holding his or her nose.

My dance routine

Create your own dance routine! Name your own dance steps and put them in the order you want (use the blocks to help). Make the dance routine short, so that you can repeat it many times. You'll also want to think of rules to start and stop the routine.

Start:
When the music starts!
When someone asks you to dance.
When you feel happy.

End:
After repeating 5 times.
When you're out of breath.
When the music stops.

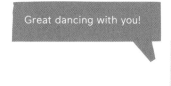
Great dancing with you!

Hint!
Can you think of things in your everyday life that are loops? School days, routines, songs?

6

THE FOXES

Working together can get messy if everyone doesn't know what to do. Ruby, being a practical girl, knows that giving clear instructions and responsibilities are just what those messy Foxes need to get the job done.

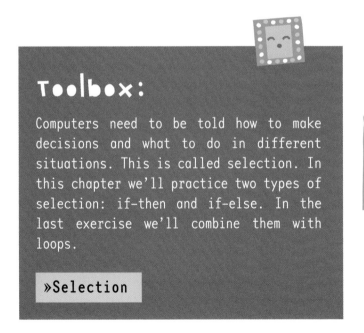

Toolbox:

Computers need to be told how to make decisions and what to do in different situations. This is called selection. In this chapter we'll practice two types of selection: if-then and if-else. In the last exercise we'll combine them with loops.

»Selection

We computers use words like *if*, *then*, and *else* to help us make decisions. *Else* is our way of saying "instead."

The All-Commanding Button

On a piece of paper, write down a command for each color. When you tap on one of the buttons (do it very professionally!), your partner should react according to your commands. How fast can you tap?

If red button tapped, do this:

If blue button tapped, do this:

If yellow button tapped, do this:

You see computer commands like these every day! When you press a button on the microwave, it warms the food for 30 seconds. If you press the button for the elevator, it will come.

 **Hint!**

Here are some ideas for commands:
Say "Woo!"
Clap your hands.
Jump up and down.
Spin around.
Say "I love you" very fast.
Tickle the other person.

Plant and Weed

The Foxes have turned Ruby's planting advice into instructions. But they've forgotten some details. Can you fill in the instructions?

Plant
Drop a seed into a hole and move one hole to the right.

Skip
Jump over one carrot to the next available hole.

Weed
Remove the bug and drop a seed into the empty hole.

0

This is how a fox would plant an entire row of carrots.

1

Now a shortcut! What's missing from the instructions?

Easy-peasy

2

One piece of instruction has gone missing. Can you figure out which one?

You'll find similar code blocks in many visual coding environments.

The foxes came up with a shorter way to write the instructions. Can you help them fill in the code?

Many things are missing from this piece of instruction. Can you figure it out?

5

You know how to do this already!

6

Oops, there's a bug in the row. What should you do to it?

Gd

7

How would you instruct the Foxes to plant this row? Pay close attention to the word *not*.

7

THE ROBOTS

When Ruby gets to bake, she's super excited! Once she learns how to bake one type of cupcake, baking another type is not that different. Let's see what Ruby can cook up with her imagination!

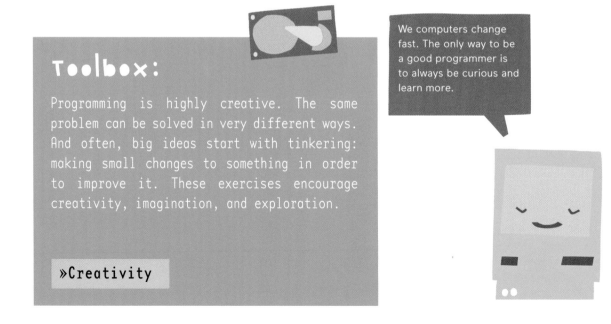

Toolbox:

Programming is highly creative. The same problem can be solved in very different ways. And often, big ideas start with tinkering: making small changes to something in order to improve it. These exercises encourage creativity, imagination, and exploration.

»Creativity

We computers change fast. The only way to be a good programmer is to always be curious and learn more.

Creative Computers

Computers are everywhere. You probably have over a hundred computers at home. No kidding! Can you help Ruby think of how the items listed here can be computers?

- How could a car be a computer?
- What about a dog?
- How can a toilet be a computer?
- What about a grocery store aisle?

Can you imagine what kinds of computers there might be in the future? And what happens to everyday objects if they have computers inside them? Take a piece of paper, draw an everyday object, and imagine what it would do as a computer.

Washing machines, burglar alarms, and microwave ovens all have computers inside them. The electrical or mechanical parts of a computer are called hardware. The instructions and the programs that run inside the computer are the software.

 You can print, build, and design your own computer at helloruby.com.

Ruby's Dress Code

Ruby is prepared for all kinds of dressing situations. Can you help her follow the rule of the yellow block to choose the right clothes to put inside the pink block? Either draw new clothes or point at the right options. (There are many!)

Example: What should Ruby wear on a rainy day?

if rainy then

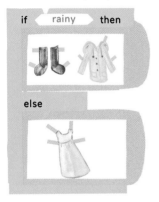

else

What should Ruby wear when baking?

if baking then

else

What will Ruby need for a day of adventure?

if adventure then

else

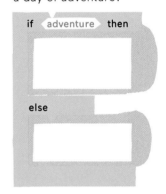

What should Ruby pack for a day at the beach?

if beach then

else

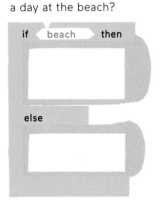

What should Ruby wear to go ice-skating?

if ice-skating then

else

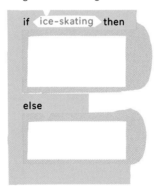

What should Ruby wear if she's not feeling well?

if not well then

else

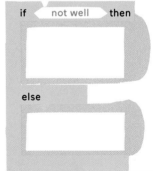

When I say *else* it means the same thing as when you say *instead*, *otherwise*, or *then*. The pink block, inside the yellow if/else block, is my way of showing instructions visually.

💡 Do it Yourself

Can you think of your own secret rule for Ruby to choose clothes? Write it on a piece of paper. Then point at one piece of clothing Ruby would wear according to your rule and one she wouldn't.

Ask a friend to point to the different clothes. You can answer whether Ruby would or would not choose those clothes. See if your friend can discover the rule!

 You can print this paper doll online at helloruby.com.

8
DJANGO

Ruby is so clever! She uses her sticks and rope in so many different ways. The next time she wants to build a raft or ladder, she'll have no problem. Now, if Ruby wants to help others build things, she can name, write down, and share her instructions.

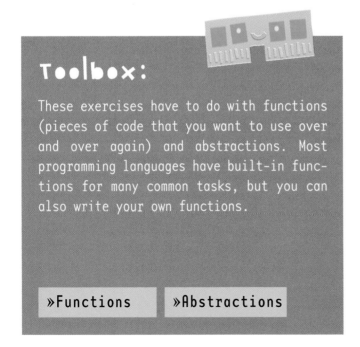

Toolbox:

These exercises have to do with functions (pieces of code that you want to use over and over again) and abstractions. Most programming languages have built-in functions for many common tasks, but you can also write your own functions.

»Functions   »Abstractions

It's good to name your functions clearly, so that you can find them easily.

Break It Down

Ruby has built a lot on her journey. See if you can put the following pictures in the right order to build things. Start by pointing to what comes first.

Can you come up with a name for each creation? This will help Ruby remember what she's built.

Name:

Align the small sticks.

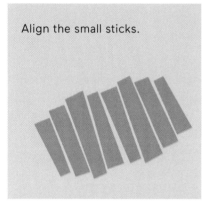

Attach the flag to the raft.

Make a flag out of the longest stick and a peice of cloth.

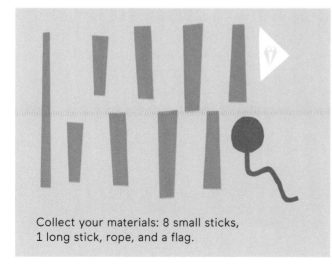

Collect your materials: 8 small sticks, 1 long stick, rope, and a flag.

Attach the sticks with rope.

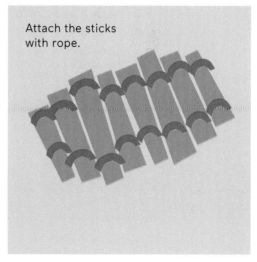

Name:

Fasten each step with rope.

Collect 5 short sticks, 2 long sticks, and some rope.

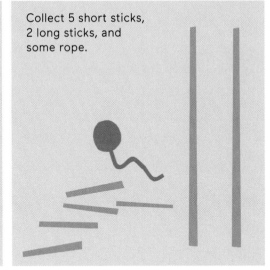

Space out the steps of the ladder.

Name:

Take cupcakes out of the oven.

Frost each cupcake with your favorite flavor.

Gather your decorations.

Drizzle decorations on top of cupcakes.

GreAt
Booya!

Ruby's Playmates

You've now met Ruby and her friends. Can you describe them? Use your imagination! Is there something all the friends could have in common?

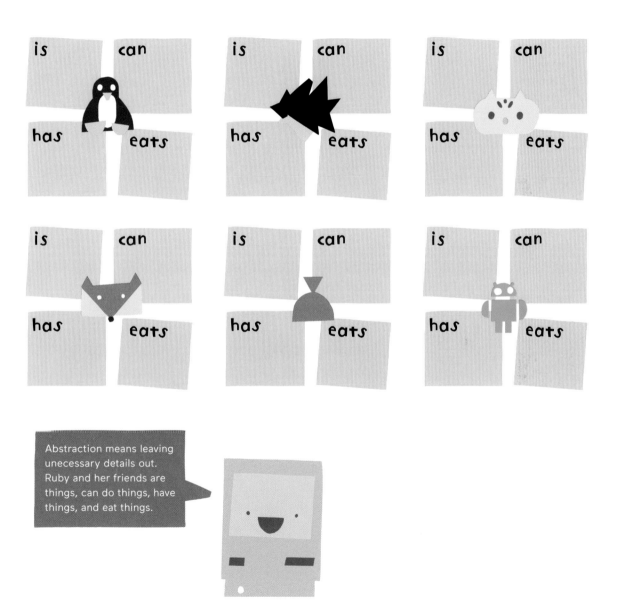

Abstraction means leaving unecessary details out. Ruby and her friends are things, can do things, have things, and eat things.

9

THE PROBLEM

New problems pop up all the time. Even though Ruby had a plan, she still failed. Luckily, Ruby doesn't give up. This is called being persistent. And asking for help is always a good thing!

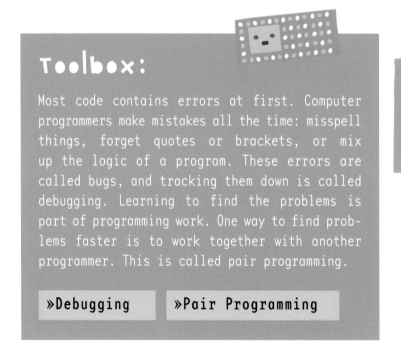

Toolbox:

Most code contains errors at first. Computer programmers make mistakes all the time: misspell things, forget quotes or brackets, or mix up the logic of a program. These errors are called bugs, and tracking them down is called debugging. Learning to find the problems is part of programming work. One way to find problems faster is to work together with another programmer. This is called pair programming.

»Debugging   »Pair Programming

Programmers care more about making the code work eventually than about trying to make the code work the very first time.

Bug Hunt

Which of these bugs are not a pair?

 Do it Yourself

Yuck! What icky bugs. Cover the bugs on this page with your hand. How many bugs are there? Can you cover all of them at once? Swipe left on top of each bug to squash them.

fAntaStic
Good work

Problems

Each of Ruby's friends has a problem. What went wrong? How would you help them?

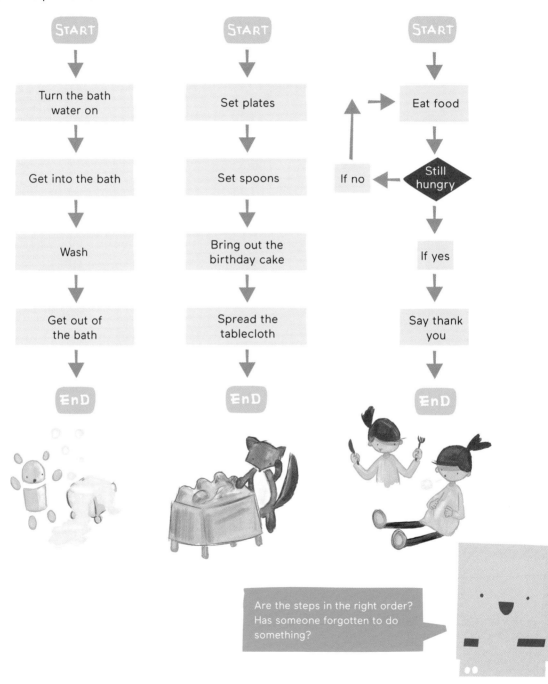

START
↓
Turn the bath water on
↓
Get into the bath
↓
Wash
↓
Get out of the bath
↓
EnD

START
↓
Set plates
↓
Set spoons
↓
Bring out the birthday cake
↓
Spread the tablecloth
↓
EnD

START
↓
Eat food
↓
Still hungry → If no
If yes
↓
Say thank you
↓
EnD

Are the steps in the right order? Has someone forgotten to do something?

Who Am I?

Can you match the right friend with the description below?

Who Am I?
- I am in the bottom row.
- I am not orange.
- I have green ears.

Who Am I?
- I have black eyes.
- I have orange in me.
- I'm not in the last two columns.

Who Am I?
- I have black in me.
- I'm not sad.
- My hair is spiky.

Who Am I?
- I have orange in me.
- I am not in the second column.
- I have a black nose.

Who Am I?
- I have round ears.
- My nose is also round.

Who Am I?
Can you write the instructions to find the missing character?

 Hint!

Sometimes it helps to read the problem aloud. Even real programmers explain their programs out loud. This is called rubber duck debugging.

10
HOME

It's been a long day of discovery. Can you use all the skills you've learned to collect the cupcakes and head back home?

Toolbox:

In this chapter we'll put it all together. We've learned about breaking a problem down into a series of sequential steps (an algorithm). And we've learned about helping the computer make decisions (selection): Do this, do that, do this or that. And finally, we've also learned about repetition (loops).

»Putting it all together

First, you'll need to think about the steps needed to solve a problem. Then, use your technical skills to get working on the problem.

LeVEL uP!

Cupcake Hunt

Now it's time for you to have an adventure with Ruby and her friends.

Preparation

The object of the game is to go and get some freshly baked cupcakes from the Robots and come back home as quickly as possible. The winner is the player who comes home first with at least one cupcake.

Each player needs one playing piece (an action figure, toy car, or other small toy). You will need one die, or you can write the numbers 1–6 on different pieces of paper and put them in a hat.

Draw 10–15 nice, small cupcake cards. Select a player who is in charge of giving out the right number of cupcake cards for each player when earned, or taking back the cupcake cards when needed.

Play

- Play rock, paper, scissors to see who goes first.
- On your turn, roll the die (or pick a number from the hat) and move your piece that number on the board. You can only move in the direction of the arrows.
- If you land on a green rectangular shape ▮ , you must follow the instructions.
- If you come upon a lilac diamond ◆ , always stop and follow the instructions.
- The first person to get to the house with at least one cupcake wins!

Do it Yourself

Design your own game! Print out the blank game board at helloruby.com and come up with your own rules.

Backpack. You didn't take your backpack with you. Go back to start and wait for your next turn.

 Penguin. STOP! You must correctly answer a true/false question asked by the player to your left. If answered correctly, take the shortcut through the Foxes' garden. If answered incorrectly, take the mountain path.

 STOP! **Snow Leopard** has a secret for you. If you roll under three, you can follow the secret path to the Robots. If you roll over three, take the longer route.

 Fox. New rule! If your token lands on this space, you get to decide a new rule for all players to follow.

Example: Every time someone rolls a two, do a Ruby dance move.

 Robots. STOP! It's a party! Roll the die. The number you roll equals the number of cupcake cards you get!

 Django. You ran into Django, who asks you to play with him. Cool! Stay and play with Django for the next two turns.

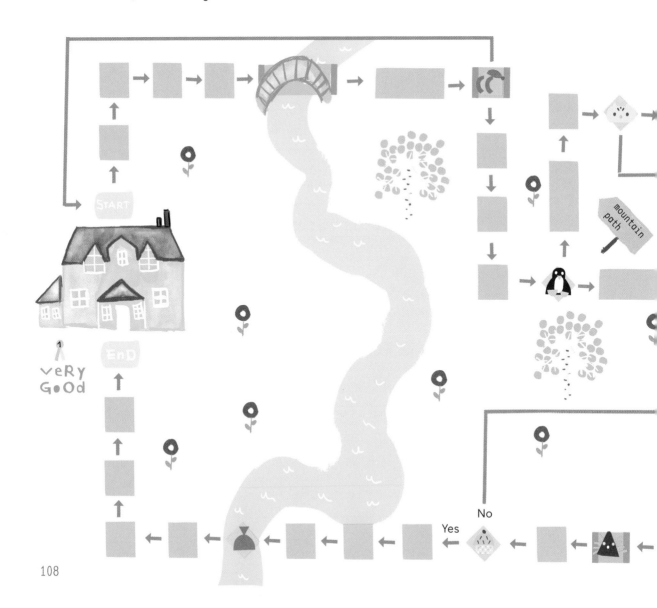

Python. Python has a challenge for you! Roll the die. If you roll an odd number, Python wins one cupcake and shares it with Django. If you roll an even number, Python lets you pass with all your cupcakes.

 Bug. Oops! Someone has taken a bite out of each of your cupcakes. You lose all your cupcakes and must give them back. Continue directly to the lilac diamond with the cupcake icon and follow its instructions.

 Cupcake. STOP! Check your cupcakes. If you have at least one cupcake left, continue on your way home. If not, return to the Robots and get new cupcakes.

 Ruby. STOP! You need to have 8 sticks for the raft over the river. The number you rolled equals the number of sticks. Keep adding the number you roll each turn, until you have collected at least 8 sticks.

 River. There's a hole in the bridge! Cross the river by rolling a four or higher.

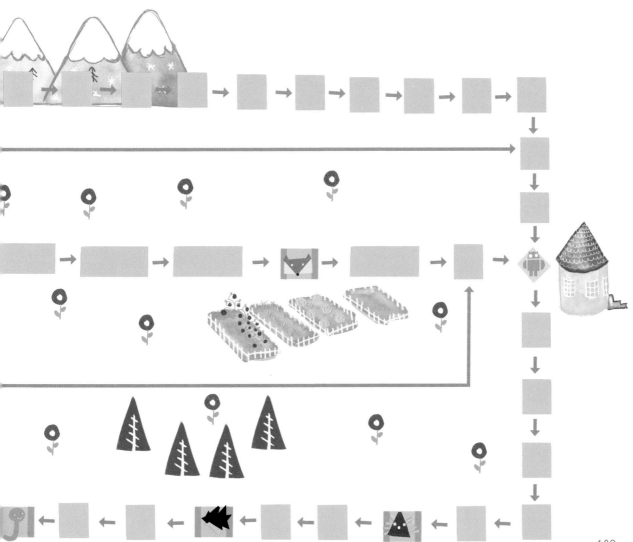

Glossary

This glossary might look like it has some big grown-up words in it, and it is mainly intended for adults. But don't get discouraged. The reason for the big words is that programmers like to be exact when talking about concepts.

Abstraction
The process of separating out details that are not needed in order to concentrate on the things that are needed. A map of the subway is an abstraction of the real, complex world. A calendar is an abstraction of your time. Even programming languages are abstractions!

Algorithm
An algorithm is a set of specific steps that you can follow to solve a problem. Ruby's plan to find the gems was an algorithm: It broke down the process of finding the gems into smaller steps. In programming, algorithms are used to create reusable solutions to problems. Search engines like Google or Bing use search algorithms to sort the results.

Booleans
Boolean expressions are things that can only have two possible answers: true or false (or 1 or 0). Boolean expressions are everywhere in computers. Computers make decisions based on whether something is true or false. Boolean logic is making statements combining expressions with words like *and*, *not*, and *or*.
NOT: If you put *not* in front of something, it becomes the opposite.
AND: If you combine two things with the word *and*, and both things are true, it means the answer is always true.
OR: If you combine two things with the word *or*, this means the answer is true when either statement is true.

Code
See *program*.

Collaboration
Working together is an important part of programming. There's even a word for it: pair programming!
One thing that has resulted from working together is open source. Open source programs allow anyone to see the code and edit it. This means a lot of different people can work on it, all over the world. Linux is one of the well-known open source projects, and Android is built using Linux code.

Ruby as a programming language is open source.
Easter eggs are tiny jokes programmers leave in their code. This book has a lot of small programmer puns. Can you find them all?

Computational thinking
Thinking about problems in a way that allows computers to solve them. Computational thinking is something people do, not computers. It includes logical thinking and the ability to recognize patterns, think with algorithms, decompose a problem, and abstract a problem.

Computer science
Computer science is the study of principles and practices of computer systems. Computer science students might study hardware, learn techniques for analyzing problems, or design data structures. Programming is one tool in the big field of computer science.

Data
Computer programs operate on data. You might know about files, like photos, videos, and games. But there's another level of data that computers understand. Programs use strings that can include letters, words, numbers, and just about any character on the computer keyboard. Another type of data is numbers. And finally, computers make decisions based on Booleans, which are statements that are either true or false. All of this data become ones and zeroes inside a computer.

Data structures
If you need to keep lots of data in one place, you can put it in a data structure. These structures are like a trunk where you can store things like numbers, strings, and other lists and change them as needed. Some of them make it *fast* to find data while others make it *easy* to sort and organize. Some of them are good at *keeping order*, or *assigning values*.

Debug
Discovering and solving mistakes in computer programs. The word *bug* originally came from a moth found in a computer in 1947 by Admiral Grace Hopper.

There are generally two types of bugs computer programmers face. First, the syntax errors, like when a programmer mistypes a word or forgets a semicolon. Second, the logic errors, where the code doesn't do the right thing.

Decomposition

The process through which problems are broken down into their smaller parts. You can decompose a meal, cupcakes, or even game levels to the parts they are made of. Programmers often break their code into smaller chunks. This makes it easier to understand and maintain.

Functions

Functions are self-contained blocks of code within a program. They allow a programmer to reuse common code blocks in different places. If you have a piece of code you use a lot, it's probably useful to make it into a function. Many programming languages also have built-in functions. In Ruby, these are called methods.

Loops

Loops are blocks of code that are repeated over and over again. Some loops run forever (infinite loops). Others have something that stops them, like counter loops that stop after they've been repeated a certain number of times or while loops that go on until the condition that stops them is met.

Pattern recognition

Finding similarities and patterns in order to solve complex problems more efficiently. To find patterns in problems, we look for things that are the same (or very similar) in each problem.

Program

A program is a sequence of instructions written in a language that the computer understands. Instructions need to be very precise or computers will make mistakes. Often, they process some kind of data to create an output.

Programming language

A language used by a programmer to write a program. There are many programming languages. Ruby, Python, and Javascript are all beginner friendly and look almost like real words. Scratch is a programming language presented in graphical blocks. Machine code looks like thousands of 1s and 0s.

Selection

Selections (sometimes called conditions) allow programmers to branch out and do one of two different options. If this something happens, do that, otherwise, do something else.

Sequence

A series of instructions that follow one another in order. Every step must be followed in sequence, after the previous step is complete. The outcome of a program will depend on the commands and how they are organized.

Variable

Variable is a place where the computer program can store one piece of data, like a number or a string. For example, in a game, the variable can store information like the score, the time left, or the user's name.

© Maija Tammi

Further, she believes that code is the twenty-first-century literacy, and the need for people to speak the ABCs of programming is imminent. She also sees our world as being increasingly run by software and sees a lack of diversity in those creating it, something that could be addressed by introducing programming to all children through compelling storytelling. Having never really outgrown fairy tales herself, she views the Web as a maze of stories and wants to hear more diverse voices in that world.

Linda has studied business, design, and engineering at Aalto University and product engineering at Stanford University. She was selected as the 2013 Ruby Hero (the most notable prize within the Ruby programming community) and is the Digital Champion of Finland.

Linda Liukas is a programmer, storyteller, and illustrator from Helsinki, Finland. The idea for *Hello Ruby* made its debut on Kickstarter and quickly smashed its $10,000 funding goal in just over three hours, becoming Kickstarter's most funded children's book in the process.

Linda is a central figure in the world of programming and is the founder of Rails Girls, a global phenomenon teaching the basics of programming to young women everywhere. The workshops, organized by volunteers in over 250 cities, have taught more than 10,000 women the foundations of programming in just a few years.

She previously worked at Codecademy, a programming education company in New York City that boasts millions of users worldwide, but left to focus on her children's book, which she believes is one of the best platforms to introduce kids to programming.

lindaliukas.fi
@lindaliukas
helloruby.com